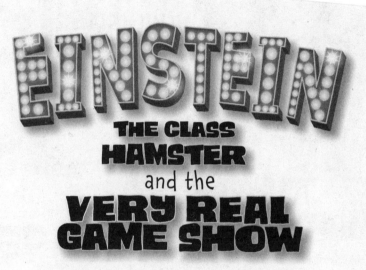

EINSTEIN
THE CLASS HAMSTER
and the
VERY REAL GAME SHOW

Janet Tashjian

TEIN

and the
VERY REAL
GAME SHOW

Illustrated by
Jake Tashjian

SQUARE
FISH

Christy Ottaviano Books

HENRY HOLT AND COMPANY ⤙ NEW YORK

SQUARE
FISH

An imprint of Macmillan Publishing Group, LLC
175 Fifth Avenue
New York, NY 10010
mackids.com

Our books may be purchased in bulk for promotional, educational, or business
use. Please contact your local bookseller or the Macmillan Corporate
and Premium Sales Department at (800) 221-7945 ext. 5442 or by
e-mail at MacmillanSpecialMarkets@macmillan.com.

Library of Congress Cataloging-in-Publication Data is available
ISBN 978-1-250-11498-3 (paperback)

Originally published in the United States by
Christy Ottaviano Books/Henry Holt and Company
First Square Fish Edition: 2017
Book designed by April Ward
Square Fish logo designed by Filomena Tuosto

1 3 5 7 9 10 8 6 4 2

AR: 4.5 / LEXILE: 680L

FOR APRIL WARD,

SUPER-GENIUS

EINSTEIN

THE CLASS HAMSTER and the VERY REAL GAME SHOW

"A person who never made a mistake never tried anything new."

—ALBERT EINSTEIN

"This was a stupid idea! What was I thinking? Help!"

—EINSTEIN THE CLASS HAMSTER

CHAPTER ONE

TIME TO COMPETE!

"**W**elcome, boys and girls, to a new episode of

ANSWER THAT QUESTION!

I'm your host, Einstein the class hamster, and we've got some great fun facts for you today. Ready, kids?"

Marlon looked around the empty classroom. Why did Einstein insist on starting each morning by talking to himself?

"Is that a yes, folks?" Einstein
asked. "Who's ready to play?"

Marlon had hoped Ned would bail
him out, but Ned was still at recess
with the rest of the class. "I'M
ready!" Marlon finally shouted.

"Our longtime champion has returned!" Einstein said into his mic. "Welcome back to the show, Marlon!"

Marlon reluctantly waved to the invisible audience.

"Marlon, here's your first question." Einstein glanced at his notes. "For fifty dollars and a chance at our

OXYMORONS:
SMALL CROWD

grand prize, is an alligator a reptile or an amphibian? You have ten seconds, and your time starts... **NOW!**"

Of course Marlon knew the answer. Alligators were reptiles, just like turtles. Einstein usually tried to make the first round a little tougher. Was this a trick question?

" FIVE SECONDS! "

Einstein called.

Maybe Einstein knew something Marlon didn't. Was there some new category alligators fell into? Did they get kicked out of the reptile group the same way poor Pluto got fired from the solar system? Maybe Marlon didn't know the answer to this question after all.

"Your time is up," Einstein said. "Care to venture a guess, Marlon?"

Marlon paced around, then took a deep breath. "Are they reptiles?"

OXYMORONS:
BAGGY TIGHTS

"Marlon, why are you answering that question with a question? **Of COURSE** alligators are reptiles, just like you." Einstein turned to face the camera, which was also nonexistent. "We'll be right back after this word from our sponsor. And stay tuned for a new Tasty Tidbit!"

Einstein scurried closer to Marlon. "Are you okay, buddy? You seem a little off your game today."

"I was confused," Marlon answered. "But everything's fine now."

"Everything's more than fine," Ned said as he approached the class pets. "Tomorrow our class competes on a national game show in front of a live audience! It's going to be great!"

Einstein tried to be happy for Ned and his other classmates, but it was hard to be enthusiastic when class pets weren't allowed on the field trip to cheer them on. He gave Ned a weak smile and changed the subject.

"Marlon just won fifty dollars in the first round of **ANSWER...THAT...QUESTION**," Einstein said. "You want to join him for round two?"

"I can't," Ned said. "I have to prepare for tomorrow."

"It's important to study," Einstein agreed.

"Oh, I'm not studying," Ned said.
"I'm figuring out a way to sneak you
into the television studio."
Einstein looked at Marlon.
Marlon looked at Einstein.
They both looked at Ned.

"The only reason our class made the finals is because you coached us," Ned said. "The class needs you there, and I'm determined to get you in."

Einstein couldn't believe the only student who could hear him was also the most dependable friend in the world. If anyone could get him into the studio tomorrow, it was Ned.

Ned bent down close to Einstein. "I'm going to try and sneak Marlon in too."

BOTH CLASS PETS? That would be amazing!

"Better rest up," Einstein told Marlon. "Looks like we might be going on a field trip."

"Is now a good time for me to

collect that fifty-dollar prize?" Marlon asked. "I **DID** win it fair and square."

But Einstein was too focused on the possibility of visiting a REAL game show.

LIGHTS! CAMERA! ACTION!

He hoped Ned and his other classmates would figure out a way to get him in.

EINSTEIN'S TASTY TIDBITS

The Crocodilia order of reptiles includes crocodiles, alligators, gharials, and caimans. They've been living on Earth for so long—more than 84 million years—that they're often referred to as living fossils. Believe it or not, their closest living relatives are birds.

... AND THEN HE SAYS, ' SEE YOU LATER, ALLIGATOR.' GET IT? GET IT?

THAT JOKE IS OLDER THAN I AM.

There are a few differences between alligators and crocodiles:

- Crocodiles' heads are much more V-shaped.
- Crocodiles are considered more aggressive than alligators.
- Crocodiles are found in countries all around the world, but alligators are found in only two: the United States and China.
- One thing crocodiles and alligators do have in common is that they're cannibals. Adults often eat young alligators and crocodiles—sometimes even their own!

UMM . . . CAN WE PLAY SOMETHING ELSE?

CHAPTER TWO

CAN NED REALLY DO THIS?

After much debate, Ned, Bonnie, and Ricky decided on the best way to sneak Einstein and Marlon into the television studio.

"I didn't know you were such a master of disguise," Bonnie told Ned. "But I still don't understand why we need to take the class pets to the game show."

"Einstein is more than a class pet," Ned answered. "And Marlon is his friend."

"Well, we're certainly going to a lot of trouble to get them in," Ricky added.

Ned couldn't tell his friends the only reason the class passed the game show audition was because of Einstein's tutoring. Sometimes Ned wished the other students could hear Einstein and

appreciate how much information
he knew from spending all his time
in classrooms. He doubted Bonnie
and Ricky would believe that Einstein
was the best study partner a kid
could have.

"Okay, class!" Ms. Moreno said.
"Tomorrow's the big day! Is everybody ready?"

The class shouted back an excited
"YES!"

LEARNING
IS
FUN-TASTIC!

"After we finish our chapter on world explorers, there are a few important details to go over about tomorrow," Ms. Moreno continued. "Such as ..." Before she could finish the sentence, Ms. Moreno fell into one of her frequent catnaps.

The students were used to Ms. Moreno falling asleep. They didn't know it, but their teacher was up most nights watching infomercials and couldn't stay awake during class. But Ms. Moreno was such a good teacher when she was awake that her students happily covered for her.

Bonnie tiptoed around Ms. Moreno and found the notes on her desk.

"The bus will leave promptly at 9 a.m.," Bonnie said. "No need to bring lunches—we'll be eating at the studio where they film the game show."

The class murmured with the excitement of free food.

"If everything goes smoothly, we'll be back at school by 4 p.m.," Bonnie continued.

"And why wouldn't things go smoothly?" Principal Decker strode

NAME 8 THINGS YOU CAN WEAR ON YOUR FEET THAT START WITH AN <u>S</u>

into the classroom with Twinkles the Python. "Why is Ms. Moreno asleep?" He snapped his fingers in front of the teacher's face to wake her up.

"We've been studying for the game show tomorrow," Bonnie answered. "Ms. Moreno hypnotized herself to memorize all those facts."

"That's what I love about Ms. Moreno—she's never afraid to try new things." Principal Decker bent down, face-to-face with the python. "Isn't that right, Twinkles?"

Twinkles nodded. (As much as a snake can nod.) He also smacked his snaky lips when he spotted Einstein and Marlon.

"Go back to the Science Center,"
Einstein said. "Nobody wants you here."

Ms. Moreno suddenly woke up and
noticed Principal Decker. "Our class has
a great chance of winning tomorrow,"
she said.

SHOES, SOCKS, SANDALS,
SNEAKERS, SKIS, SLIPPERS,
SNOWSHOES, STOCKINGS

"Well, Twinkles and I will be in the front row cheering you on." Principal Decker headed out of the room with his snake to visit another lucky classroom.

Einstein jumped up and down in a panic. "Twinkles gets to go to the TV studio? That's not fair!"

Ned agreed. *If Principal Decker can get a python into the television studio,* he thought, *then I can surely sneak in Einstein.* He looked over at Bonnie and Ricky. Plan Camouflage was officially in effect.

EINSTEIN'S TASTY TIDBITS

The Portuguese explorer Ferdinand Magellan led the first expedition around the world in 1519. Most of Magellan's crew were prisoners released from jail to help him sail under the Spanish flag. Their journey was so long, they ate sawdust, leather, and rats along the way!

Magellan was the one who gave the Pacific Ocean its name. (*Pacific* means "peaceful" and "calm.") The Strait of Magellan is named after him; it's an important passageway that connects the Atlantic Ocean and the Pacific Ocean.

This famous explorer died a tragic death in the Philippines when he was shot in the foot by a poison arrow during a fight with a local tribe. His own men retreated and left the nobleman to die alone on the beach. (Maybe prisoners don't make the best crew members after all.)

DO I HAVE A ROCK IN MY SHOE?

CHAPTER THREE
SNEAKING THROUGH SECURITY

Einstein couldn't believe Ned wasn't nervous on the bus ride to the studio. When did his shy friend turn into such a confident mastermind?

"This plan will work," Ned whispered to Einstein. "But only if you and Marlon keep perfectly still."

"Who are you talking to?" Bonnie looked around the seat and the aisle.

"No one," Ned answered a bit too eagerly.

"Here we are," Ms. Moreno said. "Victory is ours!" She stood at the bottom of the steps and waited for the class to file out of the bus.

Bonnie nudged Ned. "Suppose the security guards want to search my pack?"

"We'll be fine," Ned answered calmly.

Einstein and Marlon didn't dare move. The last thing they wanted was to get their classmates into trouble.

"Whoa! Hold up there, buddy.
What've you got there?" the security
guard asked.

Ned, Bonnie, Ricky, Einstein, and
Marlon all froze. What had given
them away?

"No animals allowed in the studio,"
the guard said. "You should know
better than that."

Ned swallowed hard. How could the class get through the show without Einstein?

But it wasn't Ned the guard was talking to. Instead, he approached Principal Decker, who was carrying a blanket over his arm.

"My school is competing on the game show," Principal Decker said. "Let me through!"

The guard whisked the blanket away, exposing Twinkles the Python.

Ned, Bonnie, Ricky, Einstein, and Marlon finally exhaled.

"**OUT!**" the security guard shouted.

"We're not going anywhere!"
Principal Decker said. (He repeated
that sentence several times while the
guard kicked him and Twinkles out.)

"That was close." Ned released
Einstein and Marlon from their hiding
places and threw his shirt into
Bonnie's pack. "Don't get into trouble."

"We'll be as quiet as a mouse,"
Marlon said.

"Mice aren't quiet," Einstein said. "They're the biggest chatterboxes in the rodent family. Seriously, they never shut up."

"As long as you do," Ned said.

But Einstein was too busy looking around to answer. He was on the set of a real game show!

KIDS KNOW STUFF

KIDS KNOW STUFF

KIDS KNOW STUFF

KIDS KNOW STUFF

EINSTEIN'S TASTY TIDBITS

The life span of a mouse is usually only one to two years—except for Mickey Mouse, who's been around for more than eight decades.

Mice are nocturnal and can't see colors; their tails are almost as long as their bodies. When they communicate with each other, they make ultrasonic noises that humans can't hear. Mice are super neat, organizing their living spaces into different areas. They're also

very smart and can find their way
through a complicated maze.

One female mouse can deliver
more than one hundred and twenty
babies each year.

CHAPTER FOUR

WE'RE REALLY HERE!

As several assistants ushered the class into the studio, Einstein and Marlon ducked behind some crates.

"Look at all the lights!" Einstein said. "And a **REAL** audience!"

"The set seems fake," Marlon complained. "It's much better on TV."

Einstein shook his head. It was generous of Ned to invite Marlon along, but let's face it—Einstein was

the one who helped the class study all those fun facts, not Marlon.

"Welcome to KIDS KNOW STUFF," the announcer boomed over the speakers. **"Here's your host, LAAAAAAAANCE WEAVER!"**

The blue curtains parted, and Lance Weaver emerged, waving to the crowd.

"It's him!" Einstein said. "The host!"

Lance Weaver was the coolest guy Einstein had ever seen—cooler than a lion tamer, engineer, and movie star combined.

"He's amazing!" Einstein crooned.

Marlon already wished he'd stayed back in the classroom.

KIDS KNOW STUFF

"Is everybody ready?" Lance asked. "Because it's time to play..."

The entire studio audience shouted along with the host, "**KIDS KNOW STUFF!**"

"Look, Marlon!" Einstein pointed to the bright words above them. "It's the APPLAUSE sign."

Sure enough, the studio audience started hooting and clapping as soon as the neon sign flashed.

"I've GOT to get one of those," Einstein said. He could already tell this was going to be the most memorable day of his life.

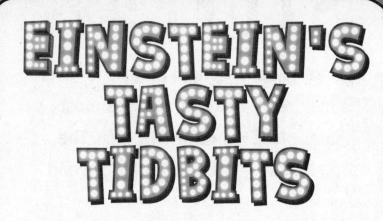

EINSTEIN'S TASTY TIDBITS

Engineer Percy Spencer was at work, standing next to a magnetron—a microwave tube used in radar systems—when he realized the chocolate bar in his pocket had melted. Percy was curious (like all good inventors), so he got some corn kernels and held them next to the magnetron, creating the first microwave popcorn. He then held up a raw egg that exploded and cooked all over his co-worker.

Percy Spencer held patents for over a hundred inventions, but he's most famous for the microwave oven. The first one he made was about five and a half feet tall and weighed 750 pounds—three times heavier than the average refrigerator!

THAT'S NOT GOING TO FIT ON THE COUNTER.

CHAPTER FIVE

MEANWHILE, IN THE PARKING LOT

"I can't believe they threw us out," Principal Decker told Twinkles. "They obviously have no appreciation for amazing reptilian specimens." He paced outside the studio until another guard came to shoo him away.

"I'm not going in without you," Principal Decker told Twinkles. "You know what the Marines say: '*Never leave a man behind*.'"

Twinkles liked being Principal
Decker's favorite pet, but the guy
was crazier than a bag of wolverines.

"There's got to be a way to get in,"
Principal Decker mumbled.

Twinkles spotted a rabbit in the

bushes behind one of the cars and licked his lips. *Come over here, little bunny. Would you like a hug?*

"I've got it!" Principal Decker said. "A surefire way into the studio!"

The principal picked up Twinkles and headed to the store at the edge of the parking lot.

The rabbit was relieved.

EINSTEIN'S TASTY TIDBITS

There's no difference between rabbits and bunnies; they're just different words for the same animal. Rabbits are herbivores that eat grasses and other plants. A rabbit's digestive system is structurally similar to a horse's; they both need to eat fibrous plants daily. It's important for rabbits to eat healthy fiber every day because, like horses, they can't vomit. For a rabbit, a hairball can be fatal.

UGH! NOT MORE FIBER!

I'LL EAT IT!

CHAPTER SIX

THIS IS IT!

Ned hoped he could harness his nervous excitement. They were going to be on television! He looked over to Bonnie, who seemed cool and collected. Ms. Moreno also appeared ready to go, her hand poised above the buzzer.

"First, the rules of the game," the host said. "Each team consists of one class and a teacher. Only two

students can compete at a time, alternating with other students in their class. Does everyone understand how to play..."

Again, the audience shouted along, **"KIDS KNOW STUFF!"**

The neon light flashed, and the audience applauded.

"So many fun facts," Einstein said. "I'd give anything to be up there."

"Let's introduce our teams," Lance continued. "Led by their teacher, Ms. Moreno, we've got students from Boerring Elementary School!"

The whole class held up their fists like boxers climbing into the ring. Einstein and Marlon cheered from the sidelines.

"Our other team is from Perfect Ed Elementary, and they're led by Mr. Tompkins!"

Ned glanced across the stage to their opponents. The teacher looked as if he'd never cracked a smile in his life, and the students looked like they ate encyclopedias for breakfast with maple syrup and toast.

"I wasn't worried before," Bonnie whispered to Ned. "But I am now."

Ned had to agree.

"Okay," the host continued. "The category is history. And our first question goes to the students from Boerring Elementary."

Ned and Bonnie got ready for the first question. Ms. Moreno gave them a big thumbs-up.

"How many Pilgrims traveled to the New World on the *Mayflower*?" Lance Weaver asked.

Bonnie suddenly looked panicked. Ned knew he'd covered this topic with Einstein during **ANSWER...THAT... QUESTION**, but with the bright lights and the studio audience staring him down, he couldn't remember a thing.

"You know this fact!" Einstein shouted from his hiding place. "We studied it last week!"

BUZZ!

Somebody pressed the buzzer.

"Boerring Elementary, what have you got?" Lance asked with a smile.

Unfortunately, Ms. Moreno's head hitting the podium was what made the buzzer buzz. The students watched their teacher snoring onstage.

Einstein's classmates needed him. There was only one thing to do. He scurried behind the stage to reach Ned.

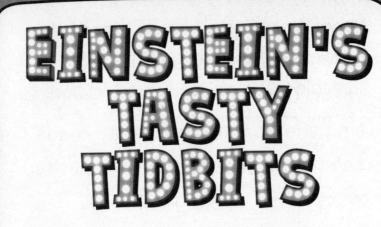

EINSTEIN'S TASTY TIDBITS

Initially, two ships were scheduled to bring the Pilgrims to America—the *Mayflower* and the *Speedwell.* But the *Speedwell* had to turn back twice because of leaks in the hull, so all the passengers were put on the *Mayflower.* The Pilgrims couldn't change their clothes or bathe for two months and were often seasick. One child was born during the journey and one child died. Believe it or not, 10 percent of all

Americans today—more than 31 million people—can trace their ancestors back to the *Mayflower* Pilgrims.

CHAPTER SEVEN

MEANWHILE, BACK AT SECURITY

The guards moved aside when they spotted the man in the silken robes and turban.

"Get out of my way!" the prince exclaimed. "Don't you know I'm royalty?"

"I'm sorry, sir. We weren't expecting you." One guard made a short bow and let the prince pass through the entry point.

"I didn't realize a real prince was coming today," the guard whispered.

He's a prince-ipal, Twinkles thought.

"Did he say he was from India?" the other guard asked.

"He sure looks familiar," the first guard added. "I've definitely seen him before."

The two guards accompanied the prince to a seat in the front row.

EINSTEIN'S TASTY TIDBITS

Many games were invented in India, including chess and Chutes and Ladders (sometimes called Snakes and Ladders). Yoga was also invented in India, as well as three of the world's major religions—Hinduism, Buddhism, and Sikhism.

CHAPTER EIGHT

WHEN THE GOING GETS TOUGH, CALL A HAMSTER

"Ned!" Einstein shouted. "How many Pilgrims were on the *Mayflower?* You can do this. Come on!"

Ned tentatively pressed the buzzer. "Ninety-nine Pilgrims?"

"I'm sorry, that's incorrect."

Why is everyone answering questions with questions? Einstein wondered.

Lance Weaver turned to Perfect Ed Elementary. Before he could repeat the question, everyone on the team hit their buzzers.

"There were one hundred and two Pilgrims traveling on the *Mayflower*," they said in unison.

"That's correct!" the host shouted.

Neither the students nor their teacher at Perfect Ed Elementary showed the slightest hint of a smile after winning the round.

"I can't believe I missed that one." Ned wished he had taken Einstein's advice and studied a little harder.

"You'll get the next one," Einstein whispered.

From the front row, Twinkles squinted toward the stage. *Is that my appetizer—I mean, my buddy Einstein?*

Principal Decker's turban slowly began to unwind.

Stay right there, my little snack.
Your pal Twinkles is on the way.

Ned noticed Twinkles sliding across the floor before Einstein did. So did a woman in the first row, who started screaming.

Several audience members jumped to their feet. Principal Decker felt his turbanless head and panicked. "Twinkles! Come to Papa!"

But Twinkles was halfway across the stage, slithering toward Einstein.

"What are YOU doing here?" Einstein said. "Go squeeze somebody your own size."

"Like you?"

Just as Twinkles was about to wind himself around Einstein, Lance Weaver leaped onto his podium, waking up Ms. Moreno.

"Call security! I'm afraid of snakes!" he screamed. "I have ophidiophobia!"

The Perfect Ed Elementary team hit their buzzers. "Ophidophobia is a fear of snakes," they all shouted.

Perfect Ed Elementary is a bunch of know-it-alls, thought Ned and Bonnie.

"Snakes are forbidden on the set. It's in my contract!" The host jumped onto a spotlight and swung across the stage. "It's either me or the snake, so I'm out of here!"

"Lance, come back!" The director turned to his assistant. "Where am I going to find a replacement host to finish the show?"

That was all Einstein needed to hear.

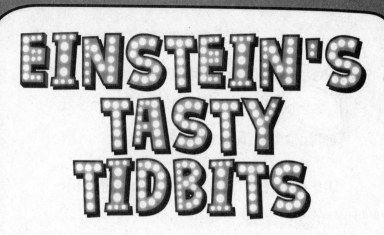

EINSTEIN'S TASTY TIDBITS

More than 19 million Americans suffer from some form of phobia. Twice as many women deal with phobias compared with men. Scientists still don't understand why certain people have irrational fears.

Here are some of the most common phobias:

- Acrophobia (fear of heights)
- Arachnophobia (fear of spiders)
- Claustrophobia (fear of confined spaces)
- Cynophobia (fear of dogs)

- Glossophobia (fear of public speaking)
- Nyctophobia (fear of the dark)
- Testophobia (fear of taking tests)

And don't forget phobophobia—the fear of phobias.

CHAPTER NINE

EINSTEIN'S TURN TO SHINE

"This is my chance to host A REAL GAME SHOW," Einstein told Marlon. "I've been preparing for this moment my whole life!"

"Then we better get you mic'd up."

Einstein looked around. It wasn't Marlon who'd answered him; it was the friendly guy standing beside him.

"You can HEAR me?" Einstein asked.

"Of course I can. I'm the sound man. You can call me Bill."

Einstein reached up to shake Bill's hand.

"Since I was a kid, I've always paid attention to sounds," Bill said. "I could tell the difference between a cardinal and a starling when I was just two years old."

"You mean when they sing?" Marlon asked.

"No. When they talk. Those birds never shut up."

"Like mice," Einstein agreed.

Marlon gestured toward Einstein. "See this hamster? He has his own game show back at school. He's a *really* good host."

Einstein couldn't hide his surprise. Marlon always seemed to be humoring Einstein when he played **ANSWER...THAT...QUESTION**. He had no idea Marlon thought he was actually good at it. Einstein really appreciated his friend's support.

"But no one in the studio will be able to hear me," Einstein told Bill.

"Except maybe you and Ned."

"You forget I'm a sound engineer," Bill answered. "By the time I get you mic'd up, everyone will be able to hear you, even the viewers at home."

This was incredible! To have people not just in the same room but all around the world listening to his Tasty Tidbits? It was too good to be true.

Einstein handed Marlon the wig and costume he'd brought along just in case.

"What am I supposed to do with these?" Marlon asked.

"Every game show host has an assistant! It'll be YOUR job to point to the prizes."

"That's not going to happen," Marlon said. "Besides there's no assistant on this game show."

"Come on!" Einstein pleaded. "Can't you just play along?"

"Sorry, Einstein. You're on your own."

Einstein begrudgingly slipped on his bow tie while Bill clipped a microphone on him. "This is a super-duper magnified mic," he said. "EVERYONE will be able to hear you." Bill called over the director. "I found a new host. You want to meet him?"

When the director asked the sound engineer if this was a joke, Einstein tried not to take it personally. He knew a hamster with encyclopedic knowledge was a lot for some people to understand.

"What are these—animatronic pets?" the director asked.

Bill gave Einstein a quick wink, then turned back to the director. "That's exactly what they are. I think the hamster will make a fun replacement host."

Einstein and Marlon tried their best to look animatronic as the director examined them. "This might be good with our kid viewers," the director finally said. "Let's give it a try."

HOW DO I LET MYSELF GET TALKED INTO THESE THINGS?

YES! "Are you SURE you don't want to join me on stage?" Einstein asked Marlon.

"Absolutely, 100 percent sure," Marlon answered.

But before he stepped into his responsibilities as host, Einstein had to share the good news with someone special.

"Ned!"

EINSTEIN'S TASTY TIDBITS

The first people who worked with animatronics were clockmakers who created characters that popped out of clocks at different hours. Leonardo da Vinci designed a mechanical lion for the King of France in 1515. Unfortunately, all that's left of the robot lion today are da Vinci's drawings.

The father of modern animatronics was Walt Disney, who created a mechanical Abraham Lincoln for the

1964 New York World's Fair. The animatronic Lincoln then moved to Disneyland, where he can be seen today. Animatronic technology has been used in lots of movies—from *Jaws* to *E.T.* to *Jurassic Park* and more.

CHAPTER TEN

BUT WHERE IS

TWINKLES?

"Twinkles! Where are you?" Principal Decker screamed as he ran through the studio.

Ms. Moreno hurried behind him. "I'm sure he's around here somewhere."

Ned broke away from the group when he heard Einstein calling.

"You'll never believe who's going to replace the host," Einstein said.

Ned's face broke into a giant smile. "You don't mean—"

"The director thinks that I'm animatronic, but everyone will find out soon enough that I'm a real live class hamster." Einstein introduced Ned to Bill the sound engineer.

"You can hear him too?" Ned asked.

"EVERYBODY'S going to hear him in a few minutes," Bill said. "Let's see if Einstein is as good as the turtle says he is."

"The name is Marlon," the turtle answered.

"Back to your places," the director called.

The only person who didn't follow the director's instructions was Principal Decker, still racing through the studio looking for Twinkles.

TWINKLES!

"Ms. Moreno and the whole class will finally know how intelligent you are," Ned told Einstein. "Not to mention everyone else in the world."

Einstein was smart enough to know that something was troubling Ned. He asked his friend what was wrong.

"If everyone can hear you, I won't be special anymore," Ned confessed. "After this, everyone will want to be your friend."

"Are you kidding?" Einstein said. "You're my BEST FRIEND. You'll always be special."

If Ned really WAS Einstein's best friend, he shouldn't be jealous. He decided to trust Einstein and let the class know how great his little buddy was.

Ned brought Einstein over to the host's podium. "Okay, let's get this show on the road."

Einstein couldn't wait to get started. He glanced at Lance

Weaver's notes—fun facts about solids and liquids, rocks and minerals, spiders and bees. All Einstein had ever wanted was to share these kinds of Tasty Tidbits with kids. His lifetime dream was about to come true.

EINSTEIN'S TASTY TIDBITS

Honeybees have been around for more than 30 million years. Bees have to visit more than 2 million flowers to make just one pound of honey, which is the primary food eaten by humans that's made by an insect. Honey is one of the only foods eaten by humans that's made by an insect and is one of the few foods that won't spoil. Honeybees perform an elaborate routine called a *waggle dance* to tell other bees where flowers are located;

when scientists studied their dances, they found the bees were giving complex information about distance and angles. Honeybees are not only dancers—they're math nerds!

CHAPTER ELEVEN

PRINCIPAL DECKER

CAUSES A SCENE

Back at their podiums, Ned leaned in toward Bonnie. "Wait until you see this! You're not going to believe it."

Bonnie pointed to the host's podium. "What's Einstein doing up there? I thought we had to hide him."

"THAT'S the surprise," Ned answered.

"But who's going to be the host?"

Ricky pointed to the other team, who hadn't budged, even through all the commotion. "We've GOT to beat these guys."

"We're definitely going to beat them," Ned said. "But I hope Ms. Moreno wakes up. She needs to see this too." He pointed to their teacher lying across the first row of the

studio audience with her arm wrapped around a woman's shoulder.

"I was just spying on the other team," Ricky said. "They're studying up on the Seven Wonders of the Ancient World. Do you think that's the next category?"

But before Ned or Bonnie could answer, the director grabbed a mic and addressed everyone in the studio. Ms. Moreno awoke with a start and scrambled back to the stage.

"We've got a little something different planned," the director said. "It's a bit of an experiment, so let's see how it goes." He looked around the set and asked the sound engineer if he was ready.

Bill nodded and began counting off for Einstein. "Five ... four ... three ..."

This is it! Einstein thought. *The moment I've been waiting for!*

"What's Einstein doing up there?" Ms. Moreno asked groggily.

"You're about to find out," Ned answered.

"ACTION!" the director shouted.

But nothing happened.

Nothing at all.

EINSTEIN'S TASTY TIDBITS

These are the Seven Wonders of the Ancient World.

- The Hanging Gardens of Babylon, *Iraq*
- The Great Pyramid of Giza, *Egypt*
- The Temple of Artemis, *Turkey*
- The Statue of Zeus at Olympia, *Greece*
- The Colossus of Rhodes, *Greece*
- The Lighthouse of Alexandria, *Egypt*
- The Mausoleum at Halicarnassus, *Turkey*

The only one of the ancient wonders still standing is the Great Pyramid of

Giza, built in 2560 B.C. The Colossus of Rhodes lasted only 56 years before it was destroyed in an earthquake. But the design lives on; that ancient wonder was the inspiration for the Statue of Liberty. "The New Colossus," a poem written by Emma Lazarus, is engraved on a bronze plaque on the Statue of Liberty's pedestal.

CHAPTER TWELVE

ANOTHER KIND OF PHOBIA

"Cut!" the director shouted. "There must be something wrong with the mic."

Ned watched as Bill adjusted the super-powerful mic clipped onto Einstein's bow tie.

"Why is Einstein here?" Ms. Moreno repeated. "And where is Principal Decker?"

Ned explained that the principal was still on the hunt for Twinkles. He hoped Ms. Moreno would focus on the snake and not on Einstein. He then hurried over to Bill to see what was going on.

"The mic seems to be fine," Bill said. "Let me do some checking." The director followed Bill to the sound board.

"I'm sorry they're having technical problems." Ned realized Einstein was shaking. "Don't worry, buddy. I'm sure they'll straighten this out."

"The only technical problem is ME," Einstein whispered. "I...I...I have stage fright."

"What are you talking about?" Ned asked. "You do this every day!"

"But never in front of a REAL audience, with REAL contestants." Einstein hated to admit the truth. "I'm scared."

Ned was surprised by Einstein's confession. Hosting a game show was Einstein's lifelong dream. How could he possibly be afraid?

"You're going to be fine," Ned reassured him. "Marlon thinks so too." He nudged Marlon forward to encourage Einstein.

"If anyone can do this, you can," Marlon said.

But Einstein just stared at his friends. He couldn't talk. He couldn't smile. He couldn't even blink.

"What are we going to do?" Marlon asked Ned. "I've never seen him like this."

Ned looked at the director and engineer examining the sound board. He had to think of something, and fast.

"I saw the snake!" Ned yelled. "Behind the director's chair!"

SNAKE!

"Where?" Principal Decker screamed.
The director jumped into Bill's arms.

"Somebody GET THAT SNAKE!"

Ms. Moreno scanned the room.
"Why are all the class pets here? You
kids have a LOT of explaining to do."
In the midst of the chaos, Ned and
Marlon snuck Einstein off the stage.

EINSTEIN'S TASTY TIDBITS

Most people forget their dreams as soon as they wake up, but some people remember them and put their dreams to good use.

Nineteen-year-old Mary Wollstonecraft Shelley came up with the idea for her novel *Frankenstein* during a dream. The plot of Robert Louis Stevenson's horror novel *The Strange Case of Dr. Jekyll and Mr. Hyde* was also formed during the author's dream. The singer/songwriter

Paul McCartney woke up from a dream with the tune to his biggest hit, "Yesterday," in his head. Elias Howe had been trying to invent an automatic way to sew but could never come up with how to thread the needle—until he had a dream about natives holding spears. The spears all had holes in their tips; when Howe woke up, he tried putting the hole at the TIP of the needle instead of the base where it had always been, thus fixing the problem and inventing the sewing machine.

So pay attention to your dreams!

CHAPTER THIRTEEN

A HEART-TO-HEART TALK

"We should've brought your tank," Ned told Einstein. "Maybe running around your wheel would help."

Einstein's friends couldn't understand his sadness. He had a big goal but today he didn't have the skill to pull it off.

"You're not quitting, are you?" Ned asked. "You're the one who always says winners never quit."

"And quitters never win," Marlon added.

"This is different," Einstein whispered. "When it comes to performing in front of a real audience, I'm a failure."

"Has anybody seen our class hamster?" Ned said. "Because THIS hamster is definitely not Einstein."

Marlon pretended to look around the room. "I think Einstein went to

get a coffee," he said. "Let's go find him."

"This IS the real me!" Einstein's heart was beating so fast, he wondered if he was having a panic attack. "I'm such a disappointment."

Ned smiled. Einstein was an expert on every subject they taught at Boerring Elementary, but today the subject he was concentrating on was drama.

"Remember when I didn't care about the class audition and you came to my house to study?" Ned asked. "You wouldn't let me give up then, and I'm not going to let you give up now."

Marlon scurried over with some sunflower seeds from the snack table. "Maybe if you eat, you'll feel better."

But Einstein was too nervous to eat.

"Let's do some relaxation exercises," Ned said. "They usually help."

As Einstein and Ned took several
deep breaths, Marlon tiptoed away.
He knew just the thing to get
Einstein excited about performing
again. But he had only a few minutes
before the director and sound
engineer returned.

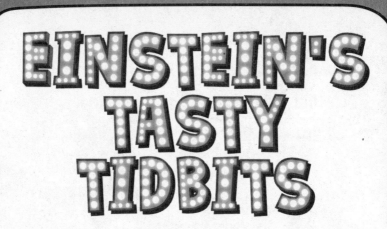

EINSTEIN'S TASTY TIDBITS

If you turned on a faucet full blast and let it run for 45 years, THAT'S how much blood your heart pumps in a lifetime—almost a million barrels. The average person's body has more than 60,000 miles of blood vessels, enough to wrap around the earth—TWICE. Only one part of the body receives no blood from the heart: the corneas in your eyes.

In 1929, Dr. Werner Forssmann put a catheter into a vein in his arm and pushed it up into his heart, inventing cardiac catheterization, a way to diagnose and treat heart conditions that we still use today. He won the Nobel Prize in Medicine for his—dangerous!—efforts.

YOU NEED ANY HELP WITH THAT?

CHAPTER FOURTEEN

BUT WHERE IS
TWINKLES?

Principal Decker heard someone scream "SNAKE," but all he saw were people scurrying around the stage. He searched the studio offices, the cafeteria, the makeup department. He searched the grocery next door as well as the gift shop. Where could Twinkles be?

The only places he hadn't looked

were the offices at the far end of the building. He ignored the flashing red light and threw open the large metal door.

Principal Decker looked around. Was this a bank? Maybe one of the tellers had seen Twinkles slither by. The poor reptile was probably disoriented and afraid.

DO NOT ENTER WHILE RED LIGHT IS FLASHING!

THIS INCLUDES YOU, SHORTY!

The principal took his place in line behind the woman with the service dog and the young man with the large bag. Principal Decker wanted to cut to the front of the line but tried his best to be patient.

When the young man got to the teller, he opened his bag and started shouting. "Everybody, down on the floor! This is a robbery!"

Principal Decker helped the blind woman next to him lower herself to the floor. Her service dog wouldn't stop barking.

ARF! ARF!

"Somebody shut that dog up," the robber yelled. "Or he's going to be sorry!"

Both the woman and Principal Decker tried to settle the dog down.

If Twinkles hadn't escaped, Principal Decker never would've ended up in this mess. But what about Principal Decker's students? What if one of them wandered away from the **KIDS KNOW STUFF** set and walked into the middle of a robbery? Principal Decker had to stop this NOW.

As the robber filled up his large bag with cash, Principal Decker whispered to the woman lying on the floor near him. "On the count of three, I'm going to rush this guy."

The woman looked afraid. "I think it's safer to just follow instructions."

"He's not going to get away with this," Principal Decker said. "Here I go! **ONE, TWO, THREE!**"

The principal transformed into sumo-wrestler mode.

"What are you doing?" The robber looked around, confused. "I told you to stay down!"

Principal Decker grabbed the man in a headlock and yelled for security. The robber squirmed, not sure what to do next.

The dog continued to bark.

"Cut!" A woman came forward from the edge of the room. "Who are you, and what are you doing? We're filming here!"

Principal Decker looked around at the cameras and lights behind him. He hadn't realized he'd wandered onto the set of a cop show. "The sign said bank," he said meekly.

"We're PRETENDING it's a bank!" the director yelled. "These are actors!" She called over the same two guards who threw out Principal Decker earlier.

The woman Principal Decker thought was blind took off her sunglasses. "You ruined that scene!" she scolded.

Even the dog looked disappointed.

EINSTEIN'S TASTY TIDBITS

Helen Keller wasn't born deaf and blind; she lost her hearing and vision after an illness when she was nineteen months old. She was the first deaf and blind person to graduate from college. Helen spent her life lecturing, writing, and advocating for people with disabilities.

Like Helen Keller, Louis Braille was not born blind; he accidentally poked himself in the eye with one of his father's tools when he was three years old. Soon, both eyes became infected, and he was blind a few days later. He became an inventor, designing the Braille method of writing in 1824 when he was just 15 years old. Braille is still used today as the primary method of reading by people who are blind.

CHAPTER FIFTEEN

BACK ON TRACK

Ned led Einstein through several breathing exercises.

"I feel much better." Einstein looked out to the game show set. "But I'm still not sure I can host."

"You HAVE to host because I'm not wearing this all day."

Einstein turned around to discover Marlon dressed as his game show assistant. He felt himself choke up.

"You'd do that for me?"

Marlon adjusted his wig. "If I'm willing to overcome my fear of wearing this silly outfit, then you need to overcome your fear of public speaking."

Bill ran over with the director.

"I checked the sound, top to bottom. The only thing left to check is the electrical system."

Einstein looked at Ned, Bill, and the director. He looked at Marlon making a huge sacrifice for him. His friends were so supportive; now it was time for him to do his part.

"We've got to finish the show," Einstein said. "I don't want to disappoint these kids."

"You really are a good friend," Ned whispered to Marlon.

"Let's get this over with," Marlon said. "These shoes are killing me."

"Okay," the director said. "Everybody, take your places!"

Ned hurried behind the podium.

"I KNOW you're up to something," Bonnie told Ned. "I just can't figure out what."

Ned leaned in to Bonnie and pointed to Einstein. "Prepare to be amazed."

"LIGHTS ... CAMERA ... ACTION!" the director called.

But all Bonnie and the others heard was silence.

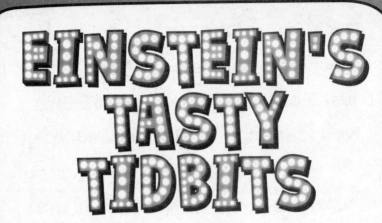

EINSTEIN'S TASTY TIDBITS

Benjamin Franklin proved that lightning is a form of electrical energy; he did NOT discover electricity. Similarly, Thomas Edison did NOT invent the first lightbulb. Heinrich Goebel did, 25 years earlier. Unfortunately for Goebel, he never applied for a patent, which would have shown that he was the inventor.

But Edison's lightbulb was an improved version of Goebel's—Edison's stayed lit longer than Goebel's bulb. Another big difference between Edison and Goebel is that Edison DID apply for a patent—1,093 of them.

CHAPTER SIXTEEN

SILENCE

Ned thought for sure that Einstein would be able to speak, especially with Marlon standing beside him giving him the evil eye. He raced to the host's podium to see what was wrong with his friend.

"It's not me this time!" Einstein said. "It's the mic. No one can hear me!"

One of the production crew hurried over to Bill. "Looks like that missing

snake got caught in the electrical panel
and burned out the circuits. Tommy is
there now trying to sedate it."

Principal Decker struggled to free
himself from the two security guards
escorting him out of the building.
"Don't touch that snake!" he shouted.
"I'm coming, Twinkles!"

The director jumped up and down like a kangaroo on fire.

"That snake has ruined this show for the last time," he screamed. "Get him off my set!"

Principal Decker raced to get to Twinkles. After a few moments, he emerged from the backstage area with Twinkles safely wrapped around him. They were both followed by a procession of serious-looking security guards who escorted them out the door.

"Can we FINALLY get back to work?" the director asked.

This is it, Einstein thought. *My destiny!*

"Thank goodness that snake's gone!" Just then Lance Weaver strolled onto the set.

NO, NO, NO! Einstein thought. *Twinkles, come back! We need you!*

The director turned to the sound engineer. "Thanks for the animatronic hamster, but we're behind schedule. Can you get Lance mic'd up?"

Bill removed the mic from Einstein. "Sorry it didn't work out, little guy. I bet you would've made a good game show host."

"A GREAT game show host!" Einstein said. "Just give me another chance!"

"No can do," Bill said. "I'm sorry."

Einstein saw the makeup person fussing over Lance to get him ready for the cameras. When Einstein turned to Ned, his best friend looked almost as sad as he did.

Marlon yanked off the wig. "This is all Twinkles's fault."

Einstein fumed. "Twinkles ruins EVERYTHING."

"Come on," Marlon said. "Let's go."
Today was a disaster for me,
Einstein thought. *But let's hope my*
classmates can still win this! He took
one last look around the stage. HIS
stage. Then he and Marlon hurried
to the sidelines to watch Boerring
Elementary compete in the final round.

EINSTEIN'S TASTY TIDBITS

Kangaroos are native to Australia and are surprisingly good swimmers. Kangaroos are marsupials, which means they give birth to immature young that finish growing in their mother's pouch. A baby kangaroo is called a joey. Joeys stay in their mother's pouch for seven to ten months—and yes, they pee and poop inside it! Kangaroo mothers must really love their joeys because they clean the pouches out by licking them.

CHAPTER SEVENTEEN

THIS IS IT!

The audience was so happy to finally have something to watch, they gave Lance a standing ovation.

"I could've had a standing ovation too," Einstein complained.

"It's better this way," Marlon said.

"How is it BETTER?" Einstein asked. "People all around the world could've discovered my game-show-hosting talents."

"Exactly," Marlon answered. "There would've been newspaper articles and interviews and talk shows. You could be president of the Game Show Hosting Association."

"President?" Einstein sighed. "And why is that bad?"

"You'd be mobbed by fans. Everyone would try to be your friend."

"Again—WHY wouldn't I want that?"

Marlon sat down next to Einstein. (His feet were still killing him from wearing those heels.) "This way you have me, you have Ned—people who really care about you."

"Don't forget Bill. He could hear me too." Maybe Marlon was right. Maybe having a few good friends who appreciated him was enough.

Einstein suddenly jumped up. "We're missing the final question!" He concentrated on sending good thoughts—and fun facts—to his classmates.

"Okay, here we go." Lance turned to the team from Perfect Ed Elementary. "How many bones are there in the body?"

The teacher, Hannibal Tompkins, hit his buzzer. "The human body? A chimpanzee body? You need to be more specific."

This guy's good, Einstein thought. *He cares about details.*

"The human body," Lance answered. "How many bones are in the HUMAN body?"

All the members of the Perfect Ed Elementary team hit their buzzers at the same time. "There are 206 bones in the human body," they answered in unison.

"Are you sure those kids are human?" Marlon asked. "They seem like robots to me."

"The answer's correct. It's 206," Einstein said. "Unless—"

Ned slapped his buzzer, which caused Bonnie to jump. "Is that an

ADULT'S body or an INFANT'S body?"
Ned asked. "Because the answer is
different."

Einstein ran in place, missing his
hamster wheel back in the classroom.
"You tell him, Ned!"

Lance fumbled with his index cards.
"Let's check in with our
judges."

"A game show host
should never be
PERPLEXED!"
Einstein complained.
"Come on, Lance!"
The director
threw off his
headset. "There ARE
no judges! We've NEVER

had judges! What are you talking about?"

"Why is the director yelling again?" Ms. Moreno yawned and looked around the set. "I had a dream all the class pets were here—"

"I think the director's having a nervous breakdown," Marlon said.

The cameraman zoomed in as the director stomped around the stage, knocking over the host's podium.

"The show is over! It's a tie! Take your prizes and go home!"

"Hey, that's not fair!" Bonnie said. "We had a real chance of winning!"

"What about our free lunch?" Ricky shouted.

The curtain suddenly flew open, revealing two sets of prizes. "An encyclopedia!" the announcer boomed. "And a Segway!"

The team from Perfect Ed Elementary rushed to the front of the stage.

"They're taking the encyclopedia!" Einstein shouted. "It's the best prize EVER. Stop them!"

"I guess we'll have to settle for the Segway," Ned said.

"An encyclopedia is a hundred times better than a Segway," Einstein said. "Everybody knows that!"

"Okay, students!" Ms. Moreno called. "Looks like we're heading back to Boerring."

Suddenly Principal Decker sprinted across the stage, followed by four security guards. "My snake!"

"My dog!" A woman's scream filled the room.

Einstein and the others stared at the very large Twinkles.

"Did he just . . . ?" Marlon asked.

"Looks like it," Einstein answered.

The guards pried the dog out of Twinkles and returned the snake to Principal Decker.

"Don't YOU ever get hungry for an afternoon snack?" the principal huffed.

The actress who'd pretended to be blind hurried to make sure the dog was okay. (He was.)

The security guards escorted the class to the bus. (Ned got to ride the Segway.) Before leaving, Einstein looked wistfully around the studio. He'd miss the lights, the fun facts, and the excitement, but not the scaredy-cat host or the cranky director. Maybe someday he'd get another chance to host a game show. Just not today.

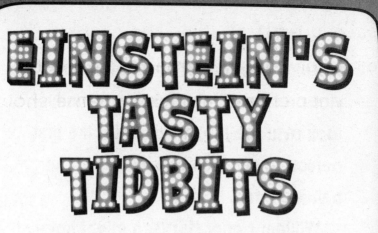

EINSTEIN'S TASTY TIDBITS

Franklin Delano Roosevelt served as president of the United States for more than 12 years, but poor William Henry Harrison served only a month in office in 1841. Harrison died of pneumonia on his 31st day as president, after doctors tried to save him with plants, opium, and castor oil.

Harrison's untimely death sparked a Constitutional debate about who should succeed him and for how long. Harrison's vice president, John Tyler, eventually took over the job, making him the first person to serve as president without being elected.

William Henry Harrison might not have done much during his month in office, but his grandson Benjamin Harrison became the 23rd president, defeating Grover Cleveland. Unfortunately for Harrison, he was defeated after one term—by Grover Cleveland, whom he beat the first time. Cleveland is the only president to serve two nonconsecutive terms.

I CAN'T DIE— I'VE GOT A COUNTRY TO RUN!

CHAPTER EIGHTEEN

BACK AT

BOERRING

As happy as Einstein was to spend the day on the set of a real game show, he was also happy to be back home in his own classroom.

Ms. Moreno buzzed around the room on the class's new Segway.

"We should've taken the encyclopedia," Einstein pouted.

"We could be reading about biomes by now. Or molecules. Or geometry."

Marlon rolled his eyes.

Ms. Moreno let Bonnie take a turn on the Segway, then hurried to the teachers' lounge. She returned with a large tray of treats.

"Cupcakes!" Ned said.

The class hurried to the front of the room, elbowing each other to get the first one.

"Turducken cupcakes!" Ms. Moreno said. "Turkey cupcakes filled with duck cupcakes filled with chicken cupcakes! I ordered special cupcake tins from the shopping network, then stayed up all night making them. Aren't they great?"

CONGRATULATIONS!

Ned and Ricky slowly put the cupcakes back on the tray.

"Eat up," Ms. Moreno said. "You deserve it!" She took a giant bite of a turkey, duck, and chicken cupcake.

"Did somebody say turducken?" Principal Decker strode into the room with Twinkles and popped one of the cupcakes into his mouth. "These are delicious."

Twinkles slithered over to Einstein and Marlon. "How about a turhammy cupcake instead?" Twinkles hissed. "A turtle inside a hamster inside a bunny?"

"Go bother someone else," Einstein said. "You've caused enough trouble for one day."

"Sorry you didn't get to host **KIDS KNOW STUFF**," Ned said. "Looks like the only game show you'll be hosting is still **ANSWER...THAT... QUESTION**."

Einstein's eyes lit up. "Do you mean NOW?"

"Of course I mean now." Ned gestured to the rest of the class,

taking turns running over cupcakes with the Segway.

"Can I play too?" Marlon asked. "You still owe me fifty bucks."

"We'll see how much of that you risk in the lightning round." Einstein hurried to his tank and looked out over the classroom.

Today might've been a disaster, but there was one question Einstein always knew the answer to: What lucky class hamster had the greatest friends in the world?

EINSTEIN!

ANSWER...
THAT...
QUESTION!

⚡LIGHTNING ROUND⚡

The students of Boerring Elementary did well on their game show. Let's see how you do.

1. True or false: Mice communicate by ultrasonic noises that humans can't hear.

2. True or false: Alligators and crocodiles are never cannibalistic.

3. Engineer Percy Spencer invented what appliance, almost accidentally?

4. Who gave the Pacific Ocean its name?

5. How many Pilgrims journeyed on the *Mayflower*?

6. Who opened the first electrical power plant?

7. What two countries are alligators found in?

8. True or false: Rabbits cannot vomit.

9. True or false: Helen Keller and Louis Braille were born blind.

10. What president served only 31 days in office?

11. Which one of the Seven Wonders of the Ancient World is still standing?

12. How many people died on the voyage of the *Mayflower*?

13. Arachnophobia is the fear of what?

14. Chess was invented in which country?

15. How do mother kangaroos clean their pouches?

16. What is the only part of the body that does NOT receive blood from the heart?

17. What do honeybees do to give one another important information?

18. What gave both Mary Wollstonecraft Shelley and Robert Louis Stevenson ideas for their horror novels?

19. What famous artist and inventor created an animatronic lion in the 1500s?

20. Who invented the FIRST lightbulb?

How well did you do?

1. *TRUE*

2. *FALSE*

3. *THE MICROWAVE*

4. *FERDINAND MAGELLAN*

5. *102*

6. *THOMAS EDISON*

7. *AMERICA AND CHINA*

8. *TRUE*

9. *FALSE*

10. *WILLIAM HENRY HARRISON*

11. *THE GREAT PYRAMID OF GIZA*

12. *ONE*

13. *SPIDERS*

14. *INDIA*

15. *BY LICKING THEM*

16. *THE CORNEA*

17. *DANCE*

18. *DREAMS*

19. *LEONARDO DA VINCI*

20. *HEINRICH GOEBEL*

SPECIAL FEATURES

BLOOPERS AND DELETED SCENES

157

162

FIND OUT MORE

Want to find out more information about my Tasty Tidbits? Explore your local library or check out these online sites:

ALLIGATORS:
sciencekids.co.nz/sciencefacts/animals/alligator.html
sciencekids.co.nz/sciencefacts/animals/crocodilealligatordifferences.html
animals.nationalgeographic.com/animals/reptiles/american-alligator/
bbc.co.uk/nature/life/Crocodilia

MAGELLAN:
bg016.k12.sd.us/Explorers/ferdinand_magellan.htm
history.com/this-day-in-history/magellan-killed-in-the-philippines
geography.about.com/od/historyofgeography/a/magellan.htm

MICE:
bestfunfacts.com/mice.html
buzzle.com/articles/facts-about-mice.html

MICROWAVES:
web.mit.edu/invent/iow/spencer.html

RABBITS:
mspca.org/programs/pet-owner-resources/pet-owner-guides/rabbit-care-
   adoption/interesting-facts-about.html

PILGRIMS:
deseretnews.com/article/705386737/Mayflower-trivia-facts-and-resources.
   html?pg=all
plimoth.org/learn/just-kids/homework-help/mayflower-and-mayflower-
   compact

INDIA:
funfactsaboutindia.blogspot.com/2009/03/10-interesting-facts-about-india.
   html
articles.timesofindia.indiatimes.com/2007-03-10/book-mark/27879998_1_
   snakes-and-ladders-board-chess-pieces

PHOBIAS:
nlm.nih.gov/medlineplus/phobias.html
library.thinkquest.org/05aug/00415/Testophobia.htm

ANIMATRONICS:
waltdisney.org/content/early-days-audio-animatronics%C2%A9

HONEYBEES:
beeright.com/fun_facts/bees.shtml
nature.com/nature/journal/v435/n7039/full/nature03526.html

SEVEN WONDERS:
world-archaeology.com/seven-wonders/7-facts-about-the-7-wonders-of-
    the-world/

DREAMS:
brilliantdreams.com/product/famous-dreams.htm
mentalfloss.com/article/12763/11-creative-breakthroughs-people-had-their-
    sleep

THE HEART:
2020site.org/fun-facts/Fun-Facts-About-the-Heart.html
facts.randomhistory.com/human-heart-facts.html

BLIND HEROES:
disabled-world.com/artman/publish/famous-blind.shtml#ixzz2HnVduWTI

ELECTRICITY:
alliantenergykids.com/EnergyBasics/AllAboutElectricity/000418
edison.rutgers.edu/patents.htm
heinrich-goebel-realschule.de/e_invention.htm

KANGAROOS:
livescience.com/27400-kangaroos.html
nytimes.com/2012/08/14/science/how-do-female-kangaroos-keep-their-
    pouches-clean.html?_r=0

WILLIAM HENRY HARRISON:
americanhistory.about.com/od/williamhenryharrison/a/ff_w_h_harrison.htm
millercenter.org/president/harrison/essays/biography/6

GOFISH

JANET TASHJIAN

What's your favorite thing about Einstein the Class Hamster?

I think the thing I love most about Einstein is that he's living in his own little world. You could say he's a bit delusional hosting a game show or thinking he should be running the classroom, but I love his determination and spunk. Jake's illustrations make me so happy; my favorites are Einstein with his hand in his pocket and his deadpan look to the camera. Einstein is one of my favorite characters, hands down.

Have you ever had a pet hamster? What sparked your imagination for Einstein's character?

We've never had a pet hamster. We've always had AMAZING dogs. *Einstein the Class Hamster* started out as a daily comic strip that Jake created while he was in middle school. He showed it to me, and I thought it was funny and original so we started playing around with the idea of making it a book. In the original drawings Einstein looked nothing like how he does now. It took several months to create the characters of Ned, Bonnie, and Ricky. Jake and I both love Einstein's demented sense of humor.

Have you ever participated in any game shows or trivia competitions?

Neither of us have ever been on a game show, but we are both mega game nerds, and play a LOT of board games. Our dining room table always has at least two games set up on it. I love trivia games; I also love doing research. Coming up with the Tasty Tidbits for the Einstein books is definitely one of my favorite parts of writing them.

What is your favorite "fun fact" in this book and why?

Hands down, our favorite Tasty Tidbit in this book is the one about kangaroos! Jake's illustration is hilarious; I laughed out loud when I first saw it. Neither of us had any idea how mama kangaroos clean their pouches.

What can readers look forward to in Einstein's next adventure? No spoilers, please!

In the next book, Einstein and his pals try to save the school library from closing because libraries are one of the most important things on the planet. We had a lot of fun with this story too. It's worth reading the book just to see Jake's hilarious drawing of the food chain. I hope this doesn't qualify as a spoiler, but candy corn plays a part in Einstein's master plan.

Do you watch any trivia game shows on TV? And if so, which one?

I don't watch a lot of trivia game shows, although Jake and I are an amazing team when we play *Hollywood Game Night*. We talk about going on it all the time. We're such movie nerds, we'd be unstoppable on that show.

What did you want to be when you grew up?

Students ask me this all the time, and I wish I had a better answer. When I was young, I was too busy playing, reading, and studying to think about career goals. I envy people who knew what they wanted to be by age ten. I was not one of them.

When did you realize you wanted to be a writer?

Several years ago I traveled around the world, and when I got back to the States, I had to fill in some forms. One asked for my occupation and I put down "writer," even though I'd never done anything more than dabble. But deep down, I always felt being a writer would be the greatest job in the world. It took me several years to make that dream a reality.

What's your first childhood memory?

I remember cooking candies in a little pan on a toy stove that I got for Christmas. I was maybe three. I'm not sure if I remember it or if I just saw the photograph so often that I think I do.

What's your most embarrassing childhood memory?

I was singing and dancing in a school assembly with my first-grade class when my shoe fell off. I kept going without the shoe, hopping around the stage—the show must go on.

What was your worst subject in school?

I always did well in school, but for some reason I forgot all my math skills and now can barely multiply. I'd love to know where all my math skills went.

What was your first job?

I've had dozens of jobs since I was sixteen—working on assembly lines, babysitting, washing dishes, waiting tables, delivering dental molds and telephone books, selling copy machines, working in a fabric store, painting houses. . . . I could fill a whole page with how many jobs I've had.

How did you celebrate publishing your first book?
By inviting my tenth-grade English teacher to my first book signing. The photo of the two of us from that day sits on my writing desk.

Where do you write your books?
Usually in my office on my treadmill desk. But because I often write in longhand, I end up writing everywhere—on the beach, in a coffee shop, wherever I am.

When you finish a book, who reads it first?
Always my editor, Christy Ottaviano. We've been doing books together for almost two decades; I consider her one of my closest friends.

How do you usually feel once you've completed a manuscript? Are you ever sad when a book you are writing is over?
Relieved! I don't really miss my characters; they're always with me.

Are you a morning person or a night owl?
I like waking up early and getting right to work. I'm too fried by the end of the day to get anything substantial done.

What's your idea of the best meal ever?
Something healthy and fresh, with lots of friends sitting around and talking. Definitely a chocolate dessert.

Which do you like better, cats or dogs?
I love dogs and have always had one. I'm allergic to cats, so I stay away from them. They don't seem as fun as dogs, anyway.

What do you value most in your friends?
Dependability and a sense of humor. All my friends are pretty funny.

Where do you go for peace and quiet?
I head to the woods. I'm there all the time. I love the beach, too.

What makes you laugh out loud?
My son. He's by far the funniest person I know.

What are you most afraid of?
I worry about all the normal mom things, like war, drunk drivers, and strange illnesses with no cures. I'm also afraid our culture is so invested in technology that we're veering away from basic things like nature. I worry about the implications down the road.

What time of the year do you like the best?
The summer, absolutely. I hate the cold.

If you were stranded on a desert island, who would you want for company?
My family.

If you could travel in time, where would you go?
To the future, to see how badly we've messed things up.

What's the best advice you have ever received about writing?
To do it as a daily practice, like running or meditation.

How do you react when you receive criticism?
My sales background and MFA workshops have left me with a very tough skin. If the feedback makes the book better, bring it on.

What do you want readers to remember about your books?
I want them to remember the characters as if they were old friends.

What would you do if you ever stopped writing?
Try to live my life without finding stories everywhere. For a job, I'd do some kind of design—anything from renovating houses to creating fabric.

What do you like best about yourself?
I'm not afraid to work.

What is your worst habit?
I hate to exercise.

What do you consider to be your greatest accomplishment?
How great my son is.

What do you wish you could do better?
Write a perfect first draft.

What would your readers be most surprised to learn about you?
I litter McDonald's trash out of my car window when I drive—KIDDING!

What is your favorite sound?
My son laughing really hard.

What is your idea of fun?
Seeing comedy or music in a tiny club.

Is there anything you'd like to confess?
I love dark chocolate.

What would your friends say if we asked them about you?
She acts like a fifteen-year-old boy.

What's on your list of things to do right now?
EXERCISE!

What do you think about when you're bored?
Story ideas.

How do you spend a rainy day?
Watching comedy.

Can you share a little-known fact about yourself?
I love to make collages.

GOFISH

JAKE TASHJIAN

Did you ever have a class hamster at school? Or a pet hamster at home?
I've never had a hamster at home, though we've always had dogs. I did have a class hamster in preschool named Sleepyhead. In my fifth-grade class there was Garfield the hedgehog, named after the comic-strip cat.

What is your favorite trivia game show on TV?
I don't really watch trivia shows, but I love the *Jeopardy!* parodies on *Saturday Night Live*. I've seen them all a million times.

SQUARE FISH

Due to severe budget cuts, the school library will be closed for the rest of the year. How is this possible? Can Einstein and his friends save the library?

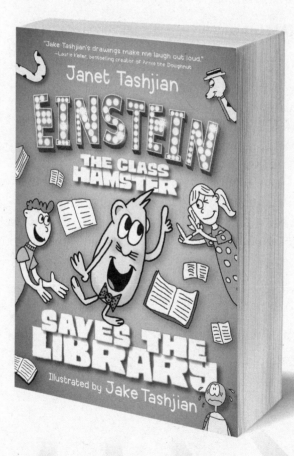

"Jake Tashjian's drawings make me laugh out loud."
—Laurie Keller, bestselling creator of Arnie the Doughnut

Janet Tashjian

EINSTEIN
THE CLASS HAMSTER
SAVES THE LIBRARY

Illustrated by Jake Tashjian

KEEP READING FOR AN EXCERPT.

Einstein pointed to Bonnie, quietly writing at her desk.

"I'm not sure she knows she's on your show today," Marlon said.

"Maybe if I command her to hear me, she'll come over." Einstein closed his eyes and concentrated on getting Bonnie to stand up. *You want to be on my game show. You can't wait to hear the latest Tasty Tidbit.*

But Bonnie continued to work.

"That went well," Marlon said.

Einstein persisted. "She's getting up! She's coming over!

I HAVE MAGIC POWERS!

"She's sharpening her pencil," Marlon said.

Einstein ignored him. "The topic of today's first round is CLOUDS. I hope all you contestants brought your umbrellas!"

Einstein watched sadly as Bonnie sharpened her pencil and returned to her seat.

"Looks like it's raining on **YOU**," Marlon said.

Show business had its ups and downs—didn't Marlon know that? And as far as "up" was concerned, nothing made Einstein happier than seeing his friend Ned, who was the only one of his classmates who could actually hear him.

"I just overheard Principal Decker talking to Ms. Moreno," Ned said. "I'm not sure what they were talking about, but it sounded like bad news."

Einstein threw himself into the pile
of shredded paper in the corner of
his tank. First Bonnie, now this?

Ms. Moreno addressed the class.
"Everyone in their seats. I have an
announcement to make."

Einstein buried himself deeper in his
paper cave.

"Pssssst!" Marlon called from his tank. "Maybe the bad news is that they're getting rid of Twinkles— maybe it's actually GOOD news."

Twinkles the Python was the scourge of Boerring Elementary. He was Principal Decker's favorite, but he spent every waking minute trying to eat the other class pets.

Einstein scurried out from his hiding place to hear what Ms. Moreno had to say.

"Our school's in a financial crisis," she said. "And Principal Decker has to make some serious budget cuts."

Einstein crossed his fingers and toes. *Please say you're getting rid of Twinkles!*

"As of today," Ms. Moreno continued, "our school library will be closed."

"**NOOOOOOOO!**" Einstein shouted.

Closing the library? Einstein couldn't imagine anything worse.

By
JANET TASHJIAN
with illustrations by
JAKE TASHJIAN

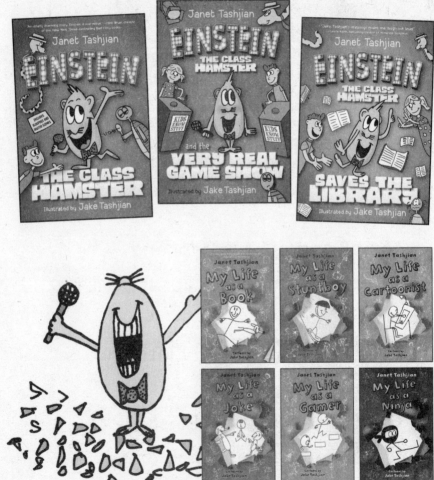